BIGGEST NAMES IN SPORTS

MAC JONES

FOOTBALL STAR

by Alex Monnig

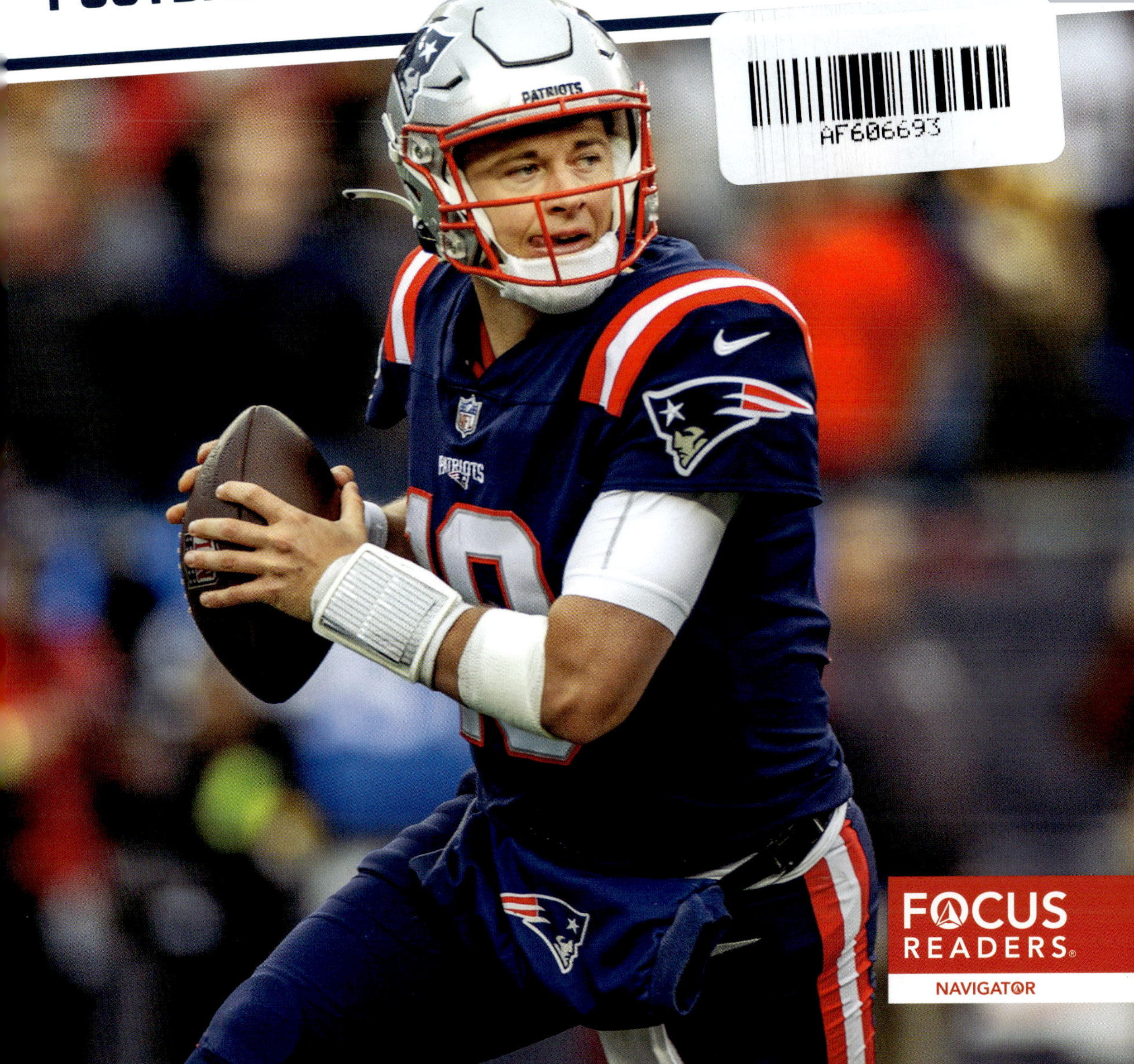

FOCUS READERS
NAVIGATOR

WWW.FOCUSREADERS.COM

Focus Readers is distributed by North Star Editions:
sales@northstareditions.com | 888-417-0195

Produced for Focus Readers by Red Line Editorial.

Photographs ©: Damian Strohmeyer/STROD/AP Images, cover, 1; Elise Amendola/AP Images, 4–5; Greg M. Cooper/AP Images, 7; Aaron M. Sprecher/CHERA/AP Images, 9; Romeo T Guzman/Cal Sport Media/AP Images, 10–11; Vasha Hunt/Alabama Media Group/AP Images, 13; John Bazemore/AP Images, 15; Rogelio V. Solis/AP Images, 16–17; Michael Woods/AP Images, 19; Peter McMahon/Miami Dolphins/AP Images, 21; Tony Dejak/AP Images, 22–23; Winslow Townson/AP Images, 25; Fred Kfoury III/Icon Sportswire/AP Images, 27; Red Line Editorial, 29

Library of Congress Cataloging-in-Publication Data
Library of Congress Cataloging-in-Publication Data is available on the Library of Congress website.

ISBN
978-1-63739-258-4 (hardcover)
978-1-63739-310-9 (paperback)
978-1-63739-411-3 (ebook pdf)
978-1-63739-362-8 (hosted ebook)

Printed in the United States of America
Mankato, MN
082022

ABOUT THE AUTHOR

Alex Monnig is a freelance writer from St. Louis, Missouri. Since graduating from the University of Missouri, Alex has covered sporting events around the world, including the Olympic Games, Rugby World Cup, Commonwealth Games, and more. He now lives in Sydney, Australia.

TABLE OF CONTENTS

NFL
PATRIOTS
10

CHAPTER 1

THE FUTURE MEETS THE PAST

Mac Jones knew the whole football world was watching. It was Week 4 of the 2021 season. Jones and the New England Patriots were hosting the Tampa Bay Buccaneers. But this wasn't an ordinary game. A Patriots legend was back in town.

Mac Jones attempts a pass during a 2021 game against the Tampa Bay Buccaneers.

Tom Brady had won six Super Bowls as New England's quarterback. Then, after the 2019 season, he left the team. He joined the Buccaneers. And in the 2020 season, he led Tampa Bay to a title.

Jones had been named the Patriots' **starter** just weeks before the 2021 season began. The **rookie** quarterback quickly showed why. Early in the second quarter, the Patriots had the ball on their own 17-yard line. Jones scanned the field. A defender sprinted toward him. But Jones calmly stepped away. Then he fired a 16-yard completion.

A few plays later, the Patriots were on the Buccaneers' 47-yard line. Once again,

Jones scans the Tampa Bay defense before taking the snap.

Tampa Bay sent heavy pressure. And once again, Jones stayed cool in the **pocket**. He hit his receiver in stride for 16 yards. On the next play, he tossed the ball out to his right for a gain of seven.

Soon, Jones had brought the Patriots to the 11-yard line. Jones took the snap and faked to his right. Defenders swarmed him. But Jones remained composed. He threw to his left for a Patriots touchdown. The stadium went wild. New England led by a score of 7–3.

The game stayed close. In the fourth quarter, Jones led a drive that resulted in a field goal. It put New England ahead 17–16 with only 4:34 to go. However, Brady led a late comeback. Tampa Bay ended up winning 19–17.

Despite the loss, Patriots fans were impressed with Jones's performance. The rookie completed 31 of 40 passes. That

Jones celebrates a great play against the Buccaneers.

included 19 in a row. Jones's calmness and decision-making reminded some people of Brady. Patriots fans hoped they were watching the beginning of another legend.

Riddell
17

CHAPTER 2

MAKING MAC

Mac Jones was born on September 5, 1998. He grew up in Jacksonville, Florida. As a kid, Mac loved going to football camps. In high school, he played for the Bolles School. Coaches liked how smart Mac was. They also appreciated that he was good at taking feedback. Off the field, Mac was a jokester. But when

Mac Jones plays on the US U-19 National Team during his senior year of high school.

game time rolled around, he was a fierce competitor. In 2016, Mac led his team to the state championship.

After high school, Jones attended the University of Alabama. The school boasted one of the best college football programs in the country. However, Jones was low on the **depth chart** when he

TEBOW TIME

Growing up, Mac's football hero was quarterback Tim Tebow. Just like Mac, Tebow grew up playing football in Jacksonville. In the late 2000s, Tebow became a star at the University of Florida. He led the Gators to two national titles. He also won the Heisman Trophy. Mac sometimes wore a wristband with BLT written on it. It stood for "Be Like Tebow."

Jones takes a snap during a 2017 practice with the Alabama Crimson Tide.

arrived on campus. For that reason, Jones didn't get any playing time in 2017.

Jones showed what he could do before the 2018 season started. Each year, Alabama holds the A-Day spring game. Crimson Tide players compete against one another. Jones was the best quarterback that day, and he helped his team win.

However, Jones still had to be patient. He served as one of Tua Tagovailoa's backups in 2018. Jones worked hard in practice and studied the playbook. But he attempted only 13 passes that season.

Jones finally got his chance to start in 2019. It happened during Alabama's eighth game of the season. The Crimson Tide was facing the University of Arkansas. Jones didn't waste any time. He threw two touchdowns in the first quarter. He added another in the third quarter. Jones missed only four passes all game. Alabama crushed the Razorbacks 48–7.

Jones looks for a receiver during a 2019 game against Duke.

Jones started three more games that season. He won two of them. That included the Citrus Bowl against the University of Michigan. Jones threw an 85-yard touchdown pass on Alabama's first offensive play. There would be plenty more fireworks to come.

10

CHAPTER 3

A CHANCE TO SHINE

The wait was finally over. Mac Jones became the Crimson Tide's full-time starter in 2020. It ended up being a season that Alabama fans would never forget. By this point, the team was used to winning. The Crimson Tide had claimed five national titles between 2009 and 2017. Usually, they relied on a strong

Jones heaves a pass against Mississippi during the 2020 season.

defense and a powerful running game. But in 2020, the Crimson Tide took a different approach. They relied on their quarterback.

Early in the season, Alabama faced a major test. The Crimson Tide squared off against the Georgia Bulldogs. Alabama was ranked No. 2 in the country. Georgia

A STAR IN THE CLASSROOM

Jones graduated from Alabama in 2019. He earned a degree in communications and got A's in every class. During the 2020 season, he completed his master's degree in sports hospitality. Once again, he got all A's. Jones was named the Academic All-American of the Year. This award is given to the year's top student-athlete.

Jones calls a play during a 2020 game against Arkansas.

was ranked No. 3. Jones threw four touchdown passes in the game. Alabama cruised to a 41–24 victory.

Jones kept it up all season long. His passing was accurate and consistent. Jones also spent hours studying opposing defenses. His hard work paid off. He threw only four interceptions all year.

Alabama's offense was nearly unstoppable in 2020. The Crimson Tide averaged more than 48 points per game. Jones broke Alabama's single-season record for passing yards. He also set a school record with 311 completions.

Alabama went undefeated during the regular season. But Jones wasn't done yet. In the national championship game, Alabama faced Ohio State. Jones threw for 464 yards. That was the most ever in a title game. Jones also recorded five touchdown passes. Alabama crushed Ohio State 52–24.

In 2020, Jones led the National Collegiate Athletic Association (NCAA)

Jones fires a pass during the national championship game against Ohio State.

with 4,500 passing yards. He had shown that he was one of the top quarterbacks in college football. Now it was time for the next step in his career. Jones was ready to turn pro.

JONES
1

CHAPTER 4

STARTING STRONG

Mac Jones was leaving Alabama as a champion. But some **scouts** weren't sure he would succeed in the National Football League (NFL). For one thing, Jones didn't run as much as other quarterbacks. His arm wasn't as strong, either.

Jones shows off his jersey after being drafted by the New England Patriots.

Even so, Jones was selected in the first round of the 2021 NFL **Draft**. The New England Patriots chose him with the 15th overall pick. Patriots head coach Bill Belichick quickly showed his confidence in Jones. Before the 2021 season started, Belichick released **veteran** quarterback Cam Newton. The message was clear. Jones was going to be the starter.

With Jones leading the offense, the Patriots started the season with a 2–4 record. Three of those losses were by six points or less. Jones learned some hard lessons. In the NFL, just a few bad plays can mean the difference between winning and losing.

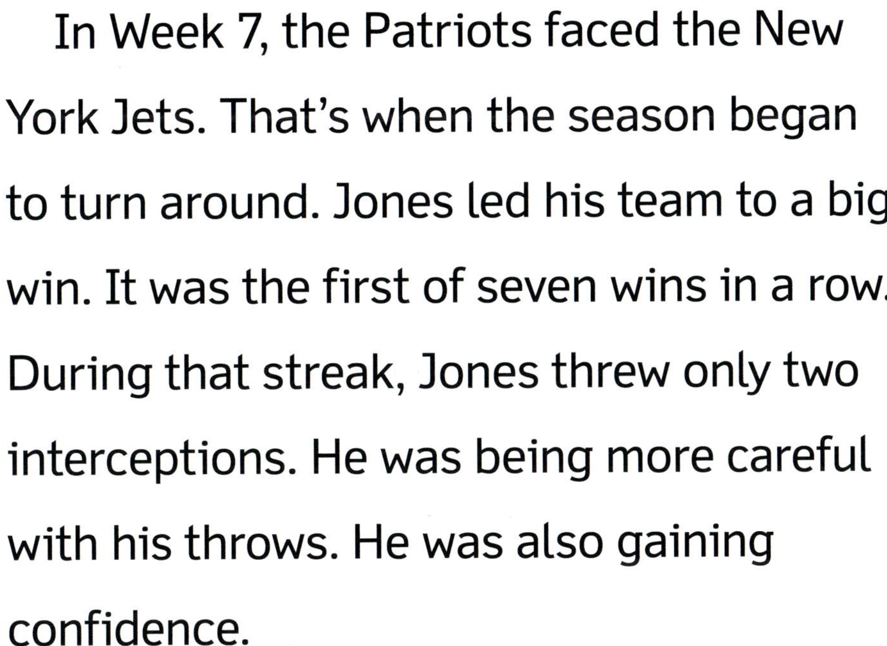

Jones attempts a pass during the first game of his NFL career.

In Week 7, the Patriots faced the New York Jets. That's when the season began to turn around. Jones led his team to a big win. It was the first of seven wins in a row. During that streak, Jones threw only two interceptions. He was being more careful with his throws. He was also gaining confidence.

In Week 12, Jones had one of his best games of the season. Facing the Tennessee Titans, Jones put up 310 passing yards. He also threw two touchdown passes in the 36–13 victory.

New England finished the regular season with a record of 10–7. That was good enough to make the **playoffs**. However, the Patriots fell to the Buffalo

PROVING THEM WRONG

Jones was the fifth quarterback selected in the 2021 NFL Draft. But he ended up having the best rookie season. He led all rookie quarterbacks in passing yards and touchdowns. His 10 wins were more than the four drafted ahead of him combined.

Jones looks for a receiver during a 2021 game against the Tennessee Titans.

Bills in the first round. Even so, Patriots fans had plenty to be excited about. With Jones leading the team, they expected more trips to the playoffs in the future.

MAC JONES

- Height: 6 feet 3 inches (190 cm)
- Weight: 217 pounds (98 kg)
- Birth date: September 5, 1998
- Birthplace: Jacksonville, Florida
- High school: The Bolles School (Jacksonville, Florida)
- College: University of Alabama (Tuscaloosa, Alabama) (2017–20)
- NFL team: New England Patriots (2021–)
- Major awards: NCAA national champion (2017, 2020); Davey O'Brien Award (2020); Johnny Unitas Golden Arm Award (2020); Manning Award (2020)

Foxborough
Tuscaloosa
Jacksonville

FOCUS ON
MAC JONES

Write your answers on a separate piece of paper.

1. Write a sentence that summarizes the main idea of Chapter 3.
2. Do you think being a backup makes it easier to succeed in the future? Why or why not?
3. Which team did Alabama beat to win the national championship in the 2020 season?
   - **A.** Georgia
   - **B.** Ohio State
   - **C.** Arkansas
4. Why didn't Jones get any playing time in the 2017 season?
   - **A.** Alabama had quarterbacks who were better than Jones.
   - **B.** Jones was too focused on becoming an NFL player.
   - **C.** Jones spent too much time studying and not enough time practicing.

Answer key on page 32.

GLOSSARY

depth chart
A team's list of players based on their skill.

draft
A system that allows teams to acquire new players coming into a league.

playoffs
A set of games played after the regular season to decide which team will be the champion.

pocket
The area behind the offensive line where the quarterback stands when throwing.

rookie
A professional athlete in his or her first year.

scouts
People whose jobs involve looking for talented young players.

starter
A player who participates in a game from its beginning.

veteran
A person who has been doing his or her job for a long time and has a lot of experience.

TO LEARN MORE

BOOKS

Glave, Tom. *Nick Saban and the Alabama Crimson Tide.* Minneapolis: Abdo Publishing, 2019.

Meier, William. *Alabama Crimson Tide.* Minneapolis: Abdo Publishing, 2021.

York, Andy. *Ultimate College Football Road Trip.* Minneapolis: Abdo Publishing, 2019.

NOTE TO EDUCATORS

Visit **www.focusreaders.com** to find lesson plans, activities, links, and other resources related to this title.

INDEX

Answer Key: 1. Answers will vary; **2.** Answers will vary; **3.** B; **4.** A